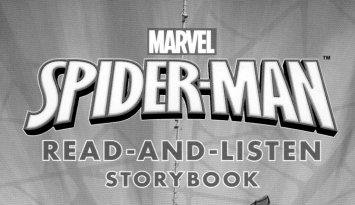

MARVEL
SPIDER-MAN™
READ-AND-LISTEN
STORYBOOK

MARVEL

New York
Los Angeles

"Spider-Man vs. Mysterio" adapted by Michael Siglain. Illustrated by Todd Nauck and Hi-Fi Design. Based on the Marvel comic book series *Spider-Man*.

"The Rhino's Rampage" adapted by Elizabeth Rudnick. Illustrated by Craig Rousseau and Hi-Fi Design. Based on the Marvel comic book series *Spider-Man*.

"Spider-Man vs. Doctor Octopus" adapted by Tomas Palacios. Illustrated by The Storybook Art Group. Based on the Marvel comic book series *Spider-Man*.

"It's Electric" based on the stories "It's Electric," written by Alison Lowenstein, and "The Sleepless Spider," written by Bryan Q. Miller. Illustrated by Rick Burchett and Hi-Fi Design. Based on the Marvel comic book series *Spider-Man* and *Spider-Woman*.

"Spider-Man at the Beach" written by Alison Lowenstein. Illustrated by Lee Garbett and Hi-Fi Design. Based on the Marvel comic book series *Spider-Man*.

"What Makes a Hero?" written by Tomas Palacios. Illustrated by Craig Rousseau and Hi-Fi Design. Based on the Marvel comic book series *Spider-Man*.

Printed in China
First Edition
1 3 5 7 9 10 8 6 4 2
ISBN 978-1-4847-0432-5
F383-2370-2-14003

marvelkids.com

CONTENTS

What **madness** is this? Do our eyes **deceive** us? Is the amazing Spider-Man really robbing the First National Bank of New York? Read on, true believers, if you dare!

Having robbed the bank, the **now-sinister Spider-Man** escaped by crawling up the side of the building!

Not even New York's finest could catch
the web-slinger in time. Spider-Man was no
longer a hero, but a **wanted criminal**!

At Midtown High, student Peter Parker and his friends were surprised to learn of Spider-Man's criminal caper.

If only Peter's friends knew that he was really Spider-Man! Peter knew that he didn't rob the bank. It must have been an **imposter**!

Peter knew that he could find out more at the **Daily Bugle**. Changing into Spider-Man, he raced across the city.

At the *Bugle*, Peter found his boss, **J. Jonah Jameson**. JJJ had always believed that Spider-Man was a **menace**.

"Parker!" JJJ yelled, holding up that morning's paper. "I need you to get a picture of Spider-Man breaking the law for the front page!"

Peter gulped. How could he prove that Spider-Man wasn't a criminal?

Just then, a strange caped figure appeared in Jonah's office! He called himself **Mysterio**.

Mysterio told JJJ that if Spider-Man wanted to learn the **truth**, he would meet the web-slinger the next morning atop the Brooklyn Bridge.

The next morning, Spider-Man swung over to the bridge. He knew it was probably a trap, but he had to clear his name!

Spider-Man found Mysterio waiting for him.

Spider-Man tried to defeat the villain, but Mysterio's strange powers and abilities were too much for him!

With a wave of his hand, Mysterio **disintegrated** Spider-Man's webs right before Spidey's eyes!

Spider-Man lunged forward, but the menacing
Mysterio **disappeared into thin air**!

Defeated, Peter returned to the *Daily Bugle*. He could hardly believe his eyes—Mysterio was shaking hands with Jonah!

JJJ was happy to hear about Mysterio's fight with Spider-Man. He didn't trust Spidey and believed Mysterio to be New York's **true hero**.

Peter had to do something! He secretly placed a small **homing device** on Mysterio's cape.

Then, as Spider-Man, Peter used the homing device to trace Mysterio to his **secret lair**!

Within minutes, Spider-Man had tracked Mysterio to a television studio in Queens, New York. Using his **spider-signal**, he startled the villain.

Inside the television studio, **Mysterio attacked Spider-Man!**

Spidey was down but not out. He still needed to know if Mysterio was the imposter who robbed the bank.

"Of course it was me," Mysterio cackled. "Who else would have the **genius** to improve upon your powers?"

21

"Once I was a great special effects and makeup artist. But then the movies changed, and effects were done on computers. No one needed classic special effects anymore . . .

". . . so I used my skills to duplicate yours. I created an entirely new character—the menacing Mysterio! And as Mysterio, I will defeat Spider-Man and become **the greatest hero the world has ever known**!

"For I am both the criminal and the conqueror, Spider-Man. Now prepare to **meet your doom**!"

Before Mysterio could strike again, Spider-Man leaped into action!

But Mysterio knew the layout of the television studio. He knew exactly how to **escape**!

Mysterio ran through the set of a science
fiction show. But he could not outrun the
amazing Spider-Man!

With all of his super-strength, Spider-Man crashed
down on Mysterio, knocking the villain out cold!

Spider-Man turned Mysterio over to the police. Then he swung by the *Bugle* to let J. Jonah Jameson know who the **real hero** was.

Later, back at Midtown High, Peter listened in as his friends read the newspaper. He was relieved to hear that they thought Spider-Man was a hero again.

DAILY BUGLE

PUBLIC ENEMY NO. 1!

SPIDER-MAN:
PUBLIC ENEMY NO. 2!

SPECIAL EDITION

And so the menacing Mysterio—with his maniacal movie magic—had been defeated by the **spectacular Spider-Man**!

Peter Parker had work to do. His Spider-Man costume had **ripped** in his last battle, and it needed to be fixed.

Suddenly, Peter heard a loud knock at the door. It was **Aunt May**.

"Um, hold on, Aunt May!" Peter shouted nervously. He had to hide the costume before his aunt saw it! He quickly changed his clothes and then threw the costume under the bed just as she walked in.

"Shouldn't you be getting ready?" his aunt asked.

Peter was confused. Then he remembered. He was supposed to have dinner at Mrs. Watson's and meet her niece, **Mary Jane**.

Soon Peter stood in Mrs. Watson's living room.
"Ah, Peter," Mrs. Watson said, "I'd like you to meet
my niece."

Peter's jaw dropped. **Mary Jane was beautiful!**

"Hi, tiger," Mary Jane said, and smiled.

Aunt May and Mrs. Watson went to start dinner. Peter was still trying to figure out what to say to Mary Jane when a news alert flashed across the television screen.

"We interrupt this program to bring you important news," the anchor announced. **"The Rhino is attacking Corona Park!"**

BREAKING NEWS ALERT

3 NEWS RHINO RAMPAGE

The Rhino was one of Spider-Man's most dangerous foes! **Alexsei Sytsevich** was a crook who had volunteered for a dangerous experiment. He'd had a strange chemical applied to his skin, which created a whole new skin on top of his—one that was as thick as a rhino's and twice as strong!

"Oh, my gosh!" Mary Jane shouted, startling Peter out of his thoughts. "Flushing Meadows is so close. **Wouldn't it be amazing to see the Rhino in person!**"

Peter smiled. That wasn't a bad idea at all. He could stop the Rhino and still go on his date with Mary Jane.

Minutes later, they arrived in the heart of Flushing Meadows, Queens. Peter realized he had to figure out a way to change into his Spider-Man costume without Mary Jane learning his secret identity!

Peter told Mary Jane that he needed to get some pictures for the *Daily Bugle*. Then he raced off to change into his Spider-Man costume!

Scaling a nearby wall, Peter scanned the area. It didn't take him long to find the large **beast**. He quickly changed his clothes and then swung down in front of the Rhino.

"If you're trying to find your way back to jail," he said, "I'd be happy to take you."

The Rhino took a step back, surprised by Spider-Man's sudden arrival. He wasn't going to get beaten again. Raising his arms, **the Rhino swung up at Spider-Man**, knocking the wall-crawler back!

The Rhino threw another punch, and Spider-Man staggered. **It was like being hit with a cement block!** Shaking it off, Spider-Man shot a web and swung out of the Rhino's reach. He needed to think of something—and fast!

The Rhino charged at the wall-crawler, who quickly jumped up, causing the Rhino to hit his head. But the Rhino just shook it off. Then, before Spider-Man could stop him, the beast landed a mighty blow and thundered off. He'd escaped—for now.

During the fight, a piece of the Rhino's hard skin had flaked off. **It was just the clue Spider-Man needed!**

Spider-Man swung over the park, looking for Mary Jane. Finally, he spotted her by the entrance.

Peter did a quick change and returned to his date.

"Did you get your pictures?" she asked.

"Yup, and I'll tell you all about it," he promised, "if you let me take you out tomorrow."

"I think that can be arranged," she said, her voice teasing.

A short while later, Spider-Man crawled through the window of **Dr. Curtis Connors's** office. Holding out his hand, Spider-Man showed the doctor a sample of the Rhino's tough skin.

"There's no way to stop him while he's protected by this," Spider-Man said. "Can you help me?"

The doctor nodded and got to work. In no time, the two created a **special chemical** that could stop the Rhino. Spider-Man coated his webs with the chemical so he would be ready for his next fight.

All Spider-Man had to do now was find his foe!

Using his powerful spider-sense, the webbed wonder found the Rhino trying to break into a nearby hospital.

The Rhino attacked Spider-Man! Spidey ducked and fired his web-shooters. It was a direct hit, but nothing happened!

The Rhino charged at Spider-Man again and the two went crashing out the window to the ground below. The special chemical finally took effect and the Rhino's tough gray skin started to dissolve.

Just then, Spider-Man delivered a powerful punch to the Rhino's jaw, knocking him out!

Later, the cops arrived to arrest the defeated Rhino. Spider-Man waited until he was sure the Rhino was captured for good and then quickly raced home for his date with Mary Jane.

Peter changed back into his regular clothes and called Mary Jane. They were going out for a night on the town. And this time, Peter hoped no Super Villains would get in the way!

For Peter Parker, working for the *Daily Bugle* newspaper could be tough. But being Spider-Man seemed to be the toughest job of all.

Peter knew what came with being a Super Hero. **Great power. Great responsibility.** And great dangers . . .

While Peter was at work, **strange experiments** were happening across town.

"That's **Doctor Octopus**," said one guard to another. "They call him that because of the special machine wrapped around his waist."

Doctor Otto Octavius was a brilliant atomic researcher. He created artificial arms that helped him handle radioactive chemicals from far away.

Suddenly, an alarm rang out and a huge **chemical explosion** rocked the lab!

Not even Octavius's robotic arms could save him from being exposed to the radiation.

Dr. Octavius barely survived the explosion. He awoke in the hospital with doctors surrounding his bed. They told him he needed to rest.

Then the doctors said that his brain had been permanently damaged by the blast. Even worse, the radiation had caused the robotic limbs to become part of his body—**forever**.

Something was not right with Octavius. The damage to his brain had caused him to go **mad**. *They're jealous of me!* he thought. *They want to keep me from my work. But I'll show them!*

Suddenly, one of the mechanical arms **moved**.

And then another. Then another. Octavius could control them with his mind!

These new arms are a part of me! I command them! he thought. *With these abilities and my brilliant mind, I'm now the most powerful person on Earth!* Now, he really *was* Doctor Octopus!

Meanwhile, Peter's boss, J. Jonah Jameson, needed pictures of Doctor Octopus in the hospital. He knew Peter was the man for the job. He always got the best photographs. Jameson didn't know how Peter did it.

Little did Jameson know that
Peter Parker would have the help of
the spectacular Spider-Man!

Spider-Man climbed up the side of the hospital. It was great being Spider-Man, Peter thought. All his adventures were easy and exciting.

But when Spidey peeked into the window, he couldn't believe his eyes. Doctor Octopus was holding the hospital workers prisoner! **Spider-Man had to do something—and fast!**

"Hold it, Doc Ock!" Spider-Man said as he crashed through the window.

Spidey dodged one mechanical tentacle, then another. But there were too many!

Doctor Octopus grabbed Spider-Man and threw him out the window to the ground below.

Then the villain made his getaway before the police could arrive.

Weak and battered, Peter took off his mask. **Spider-Man had been beaten!** His powers were not enough to stop Doctor Octopus and his tentacles. He hadn't even gotten the pictures he needed for the *Bugle*.

Peter was discouraged and sad about his defeat. He thought about what it meant to be a hero. *Sometimes heroes fall,* he thought. *But a true hero always gets back up.* Peter knew he had to try once more to stop Doctor Octopus.

Peter put on his Spider-Man outfit and tracked down Doctor Octopus's laboratory. **His spider-sense tingled!** Doc Ock had set traps for him, but Spider-Man was ready!

Large machines attacked the web-slinger, but Spidey was too fast for them. Then Doctor Octopus attacked!

Doc Ock grabbed Spider-Man with his mechanical claws. **Spider-Man was in trouble.** Would he once again be defeated by the evil Doctor Octopus?

Using all of his strength, **Spider-Man broke free from Doc Ock's mechanical claws!**

Then the amazing Spider-Man lashed out at the evil Doctor Octopus with a smashing right punch to his jaw, knocking him out!

Spider-Man had done it! He had beaten the most dangerous villain he'd ever faced. And he had gotten some great pictures, too! It was a job well done for both Peter Parker and the spectacular Spider-Man!

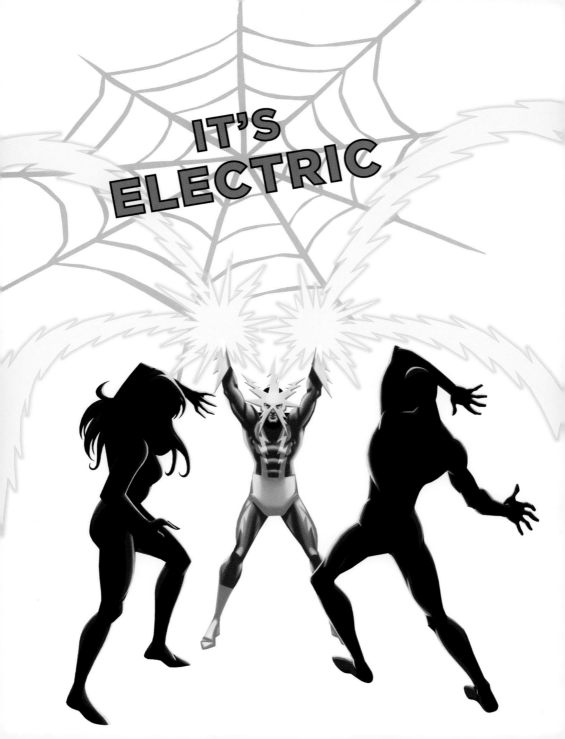

Spider-Man had been called a great many things: amazing, spectacular, sensational. But today, no matter how hard Peter Parker tried, he was none of those. **Today Spider-Man was very, very sleepy.** In fact, all he wanted to do was go home and go to bed, but there was trouble at the Policeman's Ball.

Spider-Man had been having weird dreams all week. In some, he was **back in elementary school** and had forgotten to wear his pants. In others, he was fighting the **Sinister Six**, who were winning every battle! The dreams had kept him up most of the night.

Now, Spider-Man groggily swung into action. The sinister **Shocker** was terrorizing everyone at the ball. Spidey fired his web-shooters at the villain . . . and missed! He was so tired that his aim was off.

"Look! Not only is he a menace, but Spider-Man was sleeping on the job!" J. Jonah Jameson shouted from his table as Spider-Man swung by.

But Spider-Man didn't have time to worry about
J. Jonah Jameson. **He was late for a movie night with
Mary Jane and Aunt May!** Shaking his head to wake
himself up, Spider-Man webbed Shocker's gauntlets
and knocked the vibrating villain down with a well-
timed kick.

"Maybe they won't notice I'm late," Peter said to
himself as he swung over the city a few minutes later.

"Where were you, Peter?" asked Aunt May when he returned home.

Peter held up a bowl of popcorn he had grabbed from the kitchen. "Can't have a movie night without popcorn!" he said.

Suddenly, the lights started to flicker and the TV shut off.

Peter's spider-sense was tingling. He excused himself to check the fuse box and then set out to find the culprit behind the blackout.

Meanwhile, **Jessica Drew** and her friend Lindsay were walking across the Brooklyn Bridge.

"Hey, it looks like the lights are out in the city," Lindsay said as Jessica took pictures.

Jessica, who was secretly **Spider-Woman**, had a feeling there was trouble brewing. When she saw Spider-Man swing through Manhattan, she knew she had to help. People on the bridge were pointing at the web-slinger, and Jessica was able to quietly suit up and join her fellow Super Hero without Lindsay noticing.

"Keep the lights on," Spider-Man demanded as he spotted the villain **Electro** attempting to destroy a utility pole.

"What, are you afraid of the dark?" Electro taunted as he unleashed a bolt of electricity at the wall-crawler.

Electro wanted to rob the gold vault at the Federal Reserve Bank. He was annoyed that Spider-Man was trying to save the day.

"Need some help?" Spider-Woman asked Spider-Man.

Spider-Man smiled. "Nice to see you're in town," he said. "Now that you're here, maybe I'll actually get some sleep!"

"This was supposed to be a vacation," Spider-Woman joked.

"What a treat. A Spider-Man *and* a Spider-Woman. I get to fry you both," Electro said.

"Doubtful, Electro. You had better watch your cholesterol. You're the one who is going to end up fried," Spidey told him.

Electro fired a **massive bolt of electricity** at a streetlight, causing it to short. The explosion knocked Spider-Man back!

Spider-Woman raced to confront the Super Villain, but he unleashed another powerful blast. Spider-Woman tried to block it, but she was shocked, and Electro escaped.

Electro blasted open the door to the **Federal Reserve Bank** and headed straight for the gold vault. But Spider-Man and Spider-Woman were hot on his trail.

Electro fired a massive electric burst, temporarily **blinding the heroes**, and he ran to the vault where the gold was kept.

Electro turned the large gold wheel, opening the door to the vault.

"Game over, Electro," Spidey said, shooting a web at Electro and attaching him to the wheel.

But Electro freed himself and blasted the door open. "It's not over until I have my gold," he told the Super Heroes.

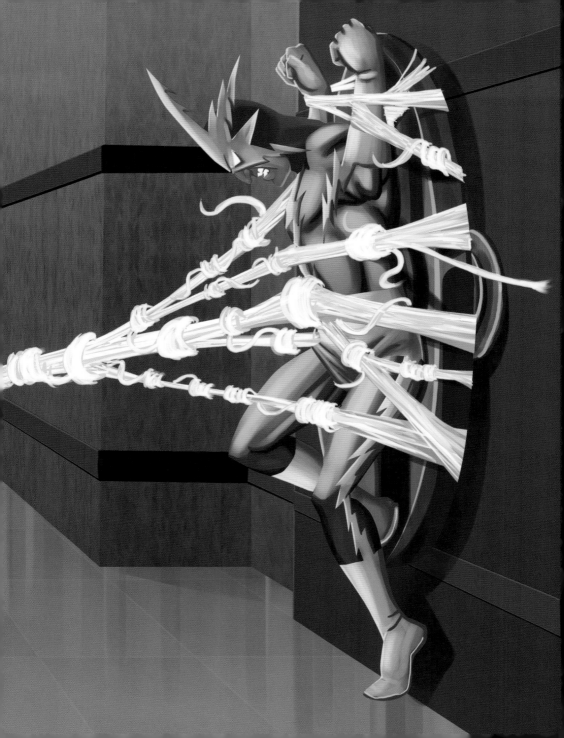

Spider-Woman knocked Electro into the vault, where he tripped and landed on the gold bricks.

Spider-Man swooped in and webbed the villain to the gold.

"Thanks for the team-up, Spider-Woman," Spidey said.

"I'm glad I was able to help. Now, I'm off to see the sights!" Spider-Woman replied as she hurried to meet her friend.

Jessica slipped beside Lindsay and began taking photos. Lindsay had been so busy looking at the city skyline that she hadn't even noticed Jessica was gone.

"Maybe tomorrow we should check out the Federal Reserve," Lindsay said, looking at her map. "I hear they offer a free tour."

"I've been there before," Jessica said with a smile. "Let's go somewhere else."

Across town, Spider-Man handed Electro over to the police and then headed home. As he swung over his neighborhood, **he was happy to see the lights coming back on**.

"Sorry it took so long," Peter said as he walked back into the living room.

"You did a great job fixing the fuse box, Peter," Aunt May said with a smile.

"You're my Super Hero," MJ said.

When the movie was over, Peter finally crawled into bed for some much-needed sleep.

He'd had a busy day. He was sure he'd have no problem sleeping tonight!

Mary Jane Watson let out a scream as she rode the Cyclone at Coney Island.

"Have you ever been on anything so terrifying?" MJ asked as she and **Peter Parker** exited the ride and walked toward the ice cream shop.

"Nope, that was scary, all right. It really goes fast for an old coaster." Peter smiled. If Mary Jane knew that he was really **Spider-Man**, and that just last night he had been swinging from the top of a skyscraper, she would know that a roller coaster didn't really scare him.

Peter and MJ got their ice cream cones and then walked toward the water. Suddenly, Peter's **spider-sense** started to tingle. In the distance, he heard a group of beachgoers shouting in alarm.

Peter looked out and saw someone in the sand. **It was Sandman**, and he wasn't making a sand castle—he was making trouble.

While MJ looked down the beach, Peter dropped his ice cream cone in the sand. Then, excusing himself to throw out the sandy cone, he quicky changed into **Spider-Man**.

"You might be made of sand, but this isn't your place in the sun," Spidey said, sneaking up on Sandman.

Sandman swung a fist at Spider-Man. "Your webs aren't strong enough to hold me!"

Suddenly, Spider-Man heard a familiar laugh. It was **Doctor Octopus**! The tentacled villain grabbed at Spidey.

"I thought I smelled something fishy," Spider-Man said, pushing Doc Ock's tentacles away.

"It's over, Spider-Man. The city is mine." Doc Ock tried to grab Spider-Man again, but Spidey jumped away.

Sandman threw another punch at Spider-Man, but Spidey avoided it. **Battling two villains wasn't easy!**

Just then, Doc Ock's tentacles grabbed hold of Spidey. **Spider-Man was stuck!** Doc Ock smiled. "There's no web you can spin that will get you out of *this*, Spider-Man."

Then Sandman got in on the action. He punched Spider-Man with all his might, knocking Spidey out of the tentacles and onto the sand.

"Look what you did!" Doc Ock yelled at Sandman. "You set him free."

"You two make a great team," Spider-Man joked as he leaped up.

Sandman raced toward the amusement park on the boardwalk. Spidey knew he was up to no good. He wanted to chase the sandy villain, but he was still trying to stop Doc Ock.

Spider-Man turned to Doc Ock. The villain had turned his tentacles into propellers and was creating a **giant wave**.

"Give up, Doc. It looks like your partner in crime is now dust in the wind. He's *desert*-ed you."

"Deserted. Very funny," Doc Ock sneered.

The waves were getting higher. Spider-Man had to do something before they flooded the beach. He shot his webs at Doc Ock, hoping to slow down his propellers.

"Stop the wind, Ock," Spidey said. "The water might be home to a real octopus, but you'll never be able to escape the waves."

Doc Ock realized that Spider-Man might be right, but he wasn't about to give up now!

With one final blast, **Spider-Man wove his webs around Doc Ock's tenatacles**. The villain fell to the ground with a thud, trapped and helpless.

"Gotcha. You're not going to slip out of this grip," Spidey said.

"Your webs will never hold me," Doc Ock said, trying to use his tentacles to break free.

"Looks like they have. You're stuck in the sun. Bet you wish you packed some sunscreen," Spidey joked.

Spider-Man swung off to stop Sandman. He found the villain stealing the money from the amusement park's ticket booths. Sandman thought Spidey was too distracted by Doc Ock to stop him.

As Sandman grabbed the money from the last booth, **Spider-Man jumped down from the Ferris wheel and leaped at him**.

"Buying a ticket to the fun house?" Spidey asked, kicking the money bag from Sandman's hand. The bag of cash fell open and the money started to blow away in the wind.

"Looks like you're blowing your money," Spider-Man said as he shot a web at Sandman.

Cornered, Sandman looked around for Doc Ock.

"If you're looking for the doctor, you're too late. He's a little tied up at the moment."

Spidey webbed up Sandman until he couldn't move, and then attached him to the Ferris wheel.

"It's your lucky day, Sandy. You get a free ride. Too bad your friend is stuck on the beach," Spidey said. Then he remembered Mary Jane. He had to find her.

As the beachgoers made their way back to the boardwalk, they cheered for Spider-Man. But Spidey wasn't thinking about all the attention; he was too concerned with finding MJ.

Finally, he spotted her in front of the ice cream shop.

"Peter, where were you?" MJ asked.

"I went to throw out my cone, and then I saw all the commotion and came looking for you."

"I was in the ice cream shop," MJ replied. "I'm so glad you're safe. Were you able to see Spider-Man?"

"I just saw him for a second. I wanted to stay out of trouble." Peter smirked.

"Want to go on some more rides?" MJ asked.

"Sure—just not the Ferris wheel," Peter said with a grin.

It had been a long week for **Peter Parker**. He had helped put out a fire, caught a jewel thief, and fought *all* of the Sinister Six.

Peter sat on a ledge and looked out at New York City. *It's not easy being a Super Hero*, he thought. *And it sure isn't easy being a teenager!*

But how could Peter Parker—or Spider-Man—rest in a city that never sleeps?

The next morning, Peter woke up in a bad mood. His body ached from the night before. He also had to finish an assignment for the **Daily Bugle** by the end of the day. *A story without Spider-Man in it?* Peter thought. *So much for an easy assignment!*

Peter grabbed his camera and headed downstairs. In the kitchen, **Aunt May** prepared a lovely breakfast and packed Peter a nice lunch. But he didn't notice. Peter trudged out the door, barely paying any attention to her.

Peter headed into New York City's Central Park. Suddenly, his spider-sense went off. A robber was stealing a woman's purse!

Peter knew he had to help. But just as he was about to change into Spider-Man . . . a hand reached out and stopped the thief. **It was a police officer!**

Peter grabbed his camera and snapped away as the police officer saved the day!

"What a great shot!" Peter said. "This will definitely make the cover of the *Bugle*. And no help from Spider-Man or *any* super powers!"

Peter looked around for more heroic pictures to take. He noticed a big brother helping his younger brother climb back onto some monkey bars.

Peter knew this too well: **when we fall, we have to get back up and try again.** Sometimes it's difficult to keep trying, but hard work pays off!

As Peter took more pictures, his spider-sense went off again. He turned to see several fire trucks racing down Fifth Avenue, their sirens blaring, their engines racing. Peter ran to the sidewalk to snap photos of **New York's bravest**. *I better change into Spider-Man and see if I can be of any service!* he thought.

Spider-Man arrived at the scene and approached an **emergency medical technician**.

The EMT smiled. "Thanks, Spider-Man, but we have everything under control," she said as she helped someone into the ambulance. "The firefighters have put out the blaze, and we are taking these people to the local hospital."

And then it hit Spider-Man. *There are other heroes!*

What makes a hero? Peter thought as he roamed the city taking pictures. *Helping others? Standing up for what is right?*

Peter made his way home and thought about all the pictures of the everyday heroes he had taken. But something was missing. **There was one hero he still needed a picture of.**

"Smile, Aunt May," Peter said.

Aunt May had done so much for Peter. She might not be everyone's idea of a hero, but **she was certainly his hero**!

The next day, Peter decided to go back to Central Park. This time, he would relax. As Peter took in the sounds and sights of the park, something caught his eye. It wasn't a thief. Or a Super Villain. . .

It was a copy of that day's *Daily Bugle*. Peter smiled.

DAILY BUGLE

DAILY BUGLE

WHAT MAKES A HERO?

WHAT MAKES A HERO?

Story by Tomas Palacios · Pictures by Peter Parker

Every day, thousands of heroes in all shapes, sizes, and colors walk among us. They are police officers and firefighters and doctors and construction workers. They are mothers and fathers and sisters and brothers. They are the people who lend a hand. They are the people who always do the right thing. They are the people who help, and they are all around us. Who knows. . . the next HERO could be YOU!

Peter learned a great lesson that day: Spider-Man can't be everywhere at once. But it's good to know that when he's not there, others will be, and that is **truly amazing**.